ROMEO

JULIET

JACK

TUMULT

For Amelia   B.F.

_____

For the Morgans of Talog   D.L.

First published 1984 by
Walker Books Ltd,
184-192 Drummond Street,
London NW1 3HP

Text © 1984 David Lloyd
Illustrations © 1984 Barbara Firth

First printed 1984
Printed and bound by
L.E.G.O., Vicenza, Italy

British Library Cataloguing in Publication Data

Lloyd, David, *1945*
Jack the dog. – (Great escapes)
I. Title   II. Firth, Barbara   III. Series
823′.914[J]   PZ7

ISBN 0-7445-0170-9

JACK

THE DOG

Written by DAVID LLOYD

Illustrated by BARBARA FIRTH

WALKER BOOKS
LONDON

'Today we go west, Jack,' Angel said. 'There's someone I want you to meet.'

They were the best of friends, the old man and his dog.

Angel had always been old, ever since Jack could remember.

He had taught Jack everything.

'Off we go, Jack,' Angel said. 'Down the bumpetty road again.'

'It's not far,' Angel said, 'just a day
and a night away.'

In the day Jack sometimes rode in the
cart, and sometimes he ran beside Angel.

In the night they slept in the open.

'There's nowhere more grand than the
Star Hotel,' Angel said, as they lay down.

Life had always been a journey like
this, ever since Jack could remember.

When they stopped the next day,
everything was the same as usual at first.
They got ready for the show.
'Bow, wow, wow! Whose dog art thou?'
Angel began, when the children arrived.

Jack barked and shook hands with Angel.
This was just the beginning.

With a huge jump, right over Angel's
back, he began the real tricks.

Jack was the cleverest dog in the world.

But after the show it was different.

Angel collected the money, like always, and packed up the cart, like always.

But then he started talking to Jack, stroking him all the time.

'I have to go away on my own now, Jack,' he said. 'I'm old, and my journey's nearly over. Nothing lasts for ever, Jack, good boy, Jack. Be clever, try to understand.'

Slowly Jack understood that Angel was saying goodbye.

They went to a house and met a man.
'This is Mr Bradley, Jack, you'll have
a good home here. He'll look after you.'
It was time for Angel to go.
'Stay, Jack,' Angel said. 'Good boy.'
So Jack stayed, because this was one
of his tricks.
And Angel went away.

There are people who are kind, and other people who pretend to be kind when they want something.

Mr Bradley only gave Jack a home because he wanted a dog who did tricks.

But when Angel went away, Jack stopped doing tricks.

He pined for the bumpetty road and the Star Hotel. He pined for Angel.

'Bow, wow, wow, Jack!' Mr Bradley said. 'Here, Jack, shake hands!'

Jack just hung his head.

'Stupid dog!' Mr Bradley said.

He made a rough kennel outside, and tied Jack there.

He brought food for Jack, but not every day.

'Stupidest dog in the world!' Mr Bradley said, aiming a kick at him.

Now Jack could only lie at the end of his rope, and watch, and wait.

Who was this looking over the wall?
Who was this climbing down?
It was Amey, from next door.
She knew Jack, she had seen the last
show, she wanted him to be free.
'Can't you escape, Jack?' she whispered.
'Can't you bite through the rope? Wait,
I'll help you. But don't make a sound,
or Mr Bradley will come!'

Jack jumped.
He really jumped like
he used to.
He almost jumped into
Amey's arms.
But he didn't make a sound.

Amey couldn't untie Jack's rope and she
didn't have a knife.

So she rubbed the rope on a brick until
it frayed, and then she and Jack pulled
together and the rope broke.

Amey tumbled over backwards.
CRASH! BANG!
She knocked over a bucket and spade.
'Quick, Jack, run!'
Amey sprang up and vanished in an
instant back over the wall.

Mr Bradley came running.

'Come here, you stupid dog!' he shouted, but of course Jack didn't come. 'I'll get you then, and heaven help you when I do!'

Now there was a chase, and Jack used all the tricks he knew. He ran rings round Mr Bradley, until Mr Bradley could run no more and just stood in the yard in a giddy muddle.

Jack jumped in the
air again, just for fun.

Then he ran round
the shed, through the
gap in the fence, and
off and away down the
bumpetty road.

Amey waved goodbye.

Jack ran and ran,
in and out of days, in and out of nights.

He slept in the Star Hotel again,
and he was happy.

He often thought about Angel.

He felt that Angel was still there, in a way.

Then one day Jack stopped running, not knowing where he was running to.

It was evening.

The stars were coming out.

A mouse and a rabbit were sitting side by side at the edge of the road.

They just looked at Jack.

'Where are you going?' the rabbit asked.

'Can we come with you?' the mouse asked.

'Please,' the rabbit said.

'We're frightened of the night,' said the mouse.

It was Tumult and Mot.

Jack found out where he was going.

He was going on, that's where, with Mot and Tumult.

'Don't worry about the night,' he said. 'I know the grandest hotel on earth.'

There are seven animals in the gang today.
They have all had great escapes.
They live together and travel together.
They are friends.
This evening they are standing on a high
hilltop. It is Jack's turn to tell the story.

'Once upon a time,' he begins, 'there was
a very wrinkled old man called Angel.'
And the story which he tells is the story
you just heard.

WALDO   LADY LOUDLY   MOT